THE GREAT FUZZ FRENZY

THE GREAT FUZZ FRENZY

Written by

JANET STEVENS and
SUSAN STEVENS CRUMMEL

Illustrated by

JANET STEVENS

Houghton Mifflin Harcourt

Boston   New York

"Violet!. No!"

"WOOF!"

Illustrations in this book were done in mixed media on watercolor paper.
The display type was set in OPTIFantastik.
The text type was set in OPTIMajerIrregular.

www.hmhco.com

The Library of Congress has cataloged the hardcover edition as follows:
Stevens, Janet.
The Great Fuzz Frenzy/written by Janet Stevens and Susan Stevens Crummel;
illustrated by Janet Stevens.
p. cm.
Summary: When a tennis ball lands in a prairie-dog town, the residents find that
their newfound frenzy for fuzz creates a fiasco. [1.Prairie dogs—Fiction. 2. Balls
(Sporting goods)—Fiction. 3. Greed—Fiction. 4 Humorous stories.]
I. Crummel, Susan Stevens. II. Title.
PZ7.S84453Fu 2005
[E]—dc22   2004022063

ISBN: 978-0-15-204626-2 hardcover
ISBN: 978-0-544-94391-9 paperback

Manufactured in China
SCP 15 14 13 12 11 10 9
4500792194

For my fellow fuzz-pickers:
Ted, Lindsey,
Dani, and Jackie
—J.S.

For my husband, Richard,
who has laughed at my jokes
for more than thirty years
—S.S.C.

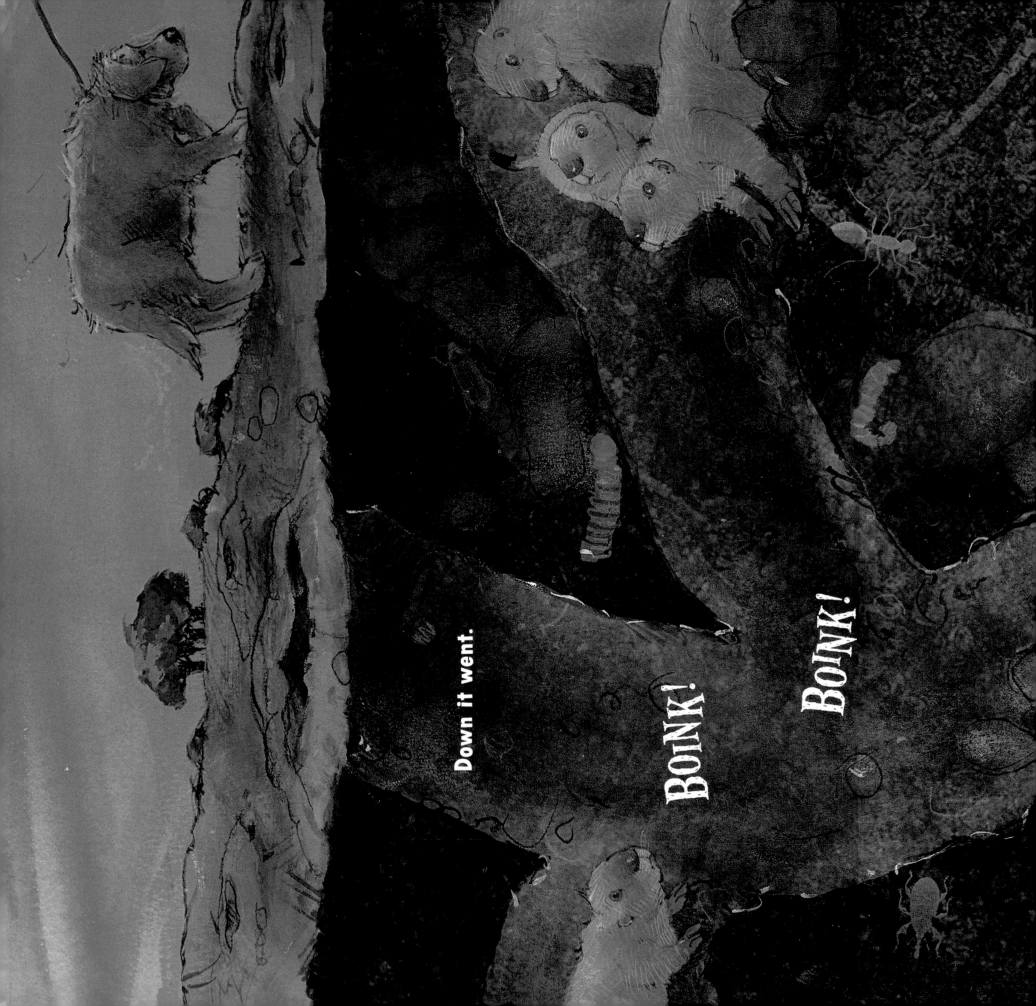

PLUNK.

There it sat—perfectly still.
The prairie dogs waited—perfectly still.

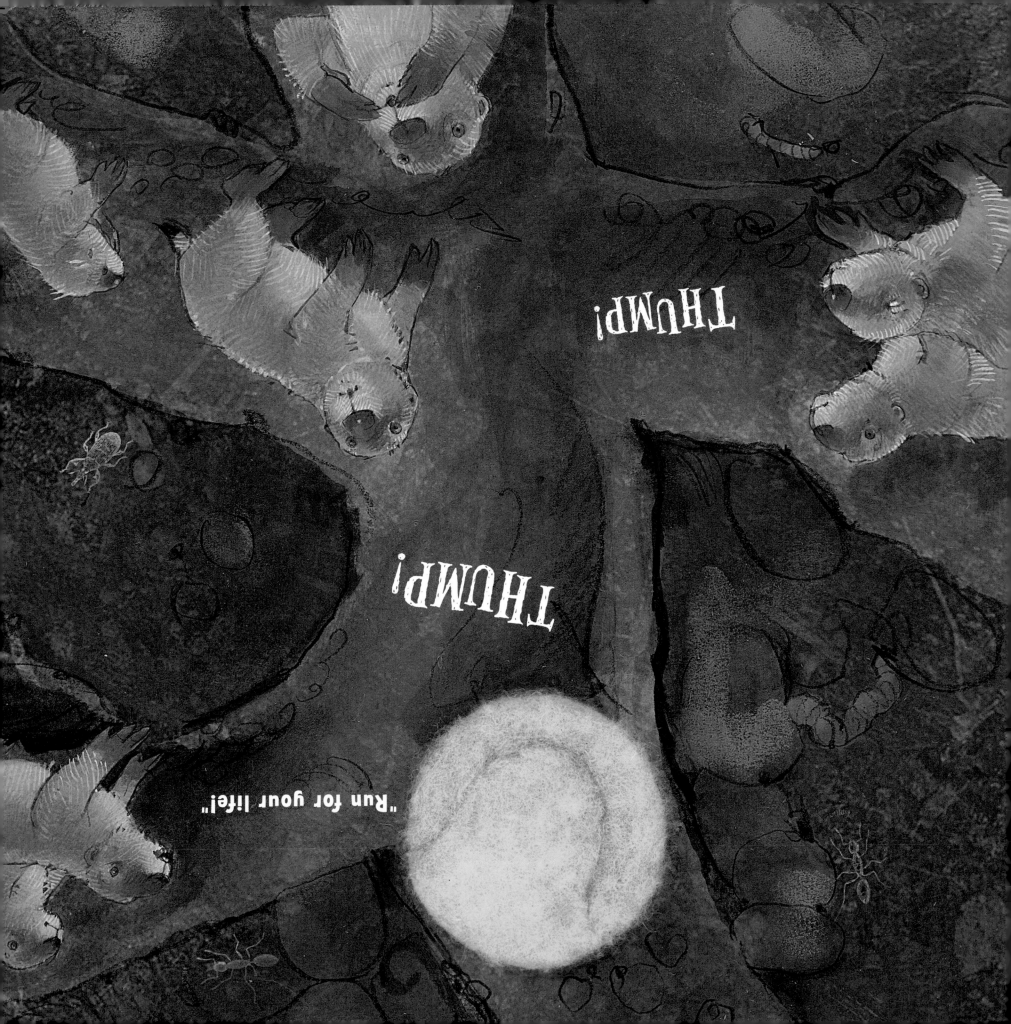

Slowly they crept out.   Inch by inch. Dog by dog.

"What is it?"

"A thing."

"A good thing or a bad thing?"

"A round thing."

"A strange thing."

"A scary thing."

"What should we do?"

"Don't touch it!"

"Is it alive?"

"Ssshhh!"

"Stand back!" boomed a voice. "You act like gutless groundhogs—afraid of your own shadow!"

"Oh no, it's Big Bark!"

"Big *Mouth* is more like it."

"He's the meanest dog around."

"I thought he left town."

"Well, I'm back," growled Big Bark. "So out of my way. Let me have a look."

But before anyone could move, little Pip Squeak raced past
Big Bark, reached out, and poked the big round thing.
"Noooooo!" the crowd yelled.
"It's fuzzy!" said Pip.
"Oooooooh!" the crowd gasped.

A tiny piece of fuzz was caught in Pip's claw.
She looked at it. Turned it. Sniffed it. Then she
put it on her head. "Look at me!"
"Ahhhhhh!" the crowd sighed.
"Quit hammin' it up, you half-pint hamster!"
snarled Big Bark. "*I'm* in charge."

But those prairie dogs didn't listen. They had to have fuzz.

"I like it."

"Me, too."   "Oh yes!"

"I want some."   "So do I!"

"Do you?"   "So do we!"

"So do they!"

"Big Bark, move over!"

"Get out of our way!"

They charged past him
and grabbed at the fuzz.

The prairie dogs pulled it. Puffed it.

Stretched it. Fluffed it.

Tugged it. Twirled it.

Spiked it. Swirled it.

They fuzzed their ears, their heads, their noses.

They fuzzed their feet, their tails, their toeses.

Big Bark was beside himself. "Listen to me, you ridiculous rodents! Stop this fuzzy foolishness!"

But those prairie dogs didn't listen.
They were busy being hot dogs and silly dogs.
Corny dogs and frilly dogs.
Top dogs. Funny dogs.
Superdogs. Bunny dogs.

"You're all nuts, you squirrelly fuzz freaks!" yelled Big Bark, storming off.

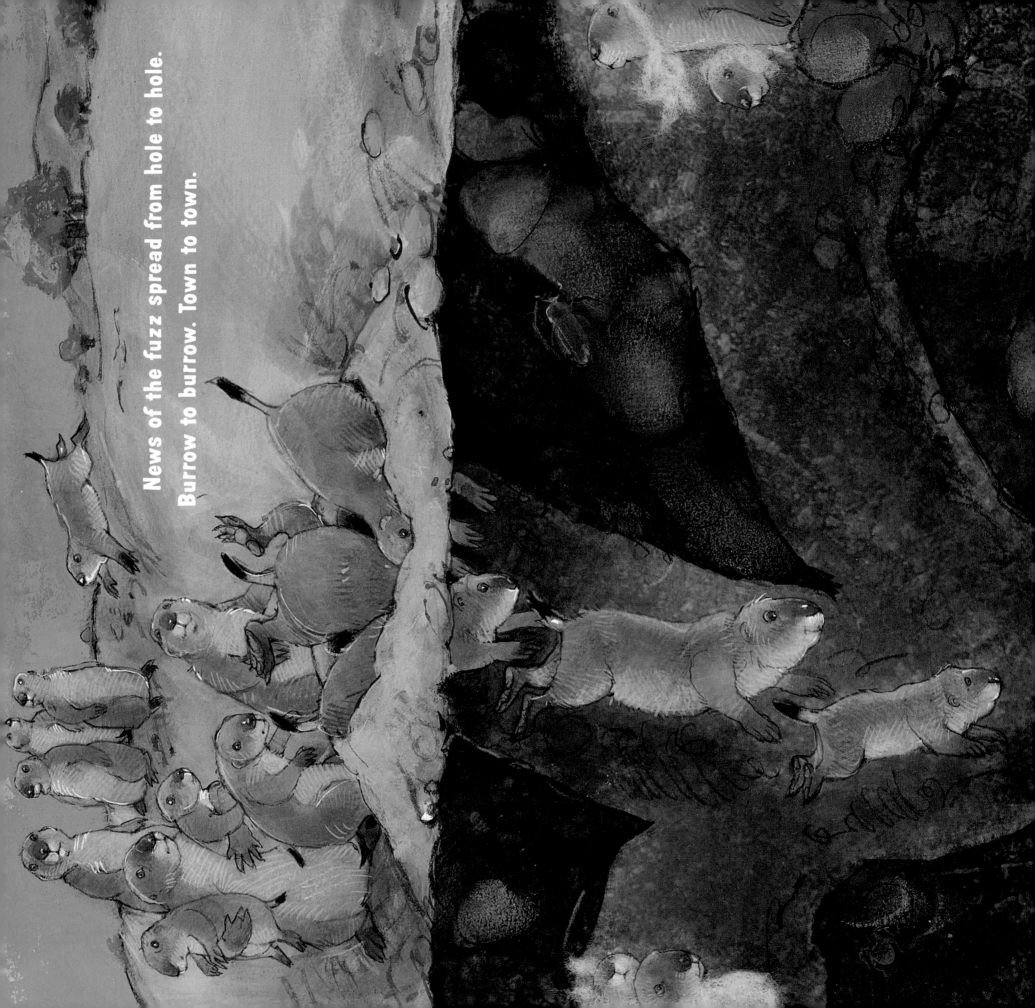

News of the fuzz spread from hole to hole.
Burrow to burrow. Town to town.

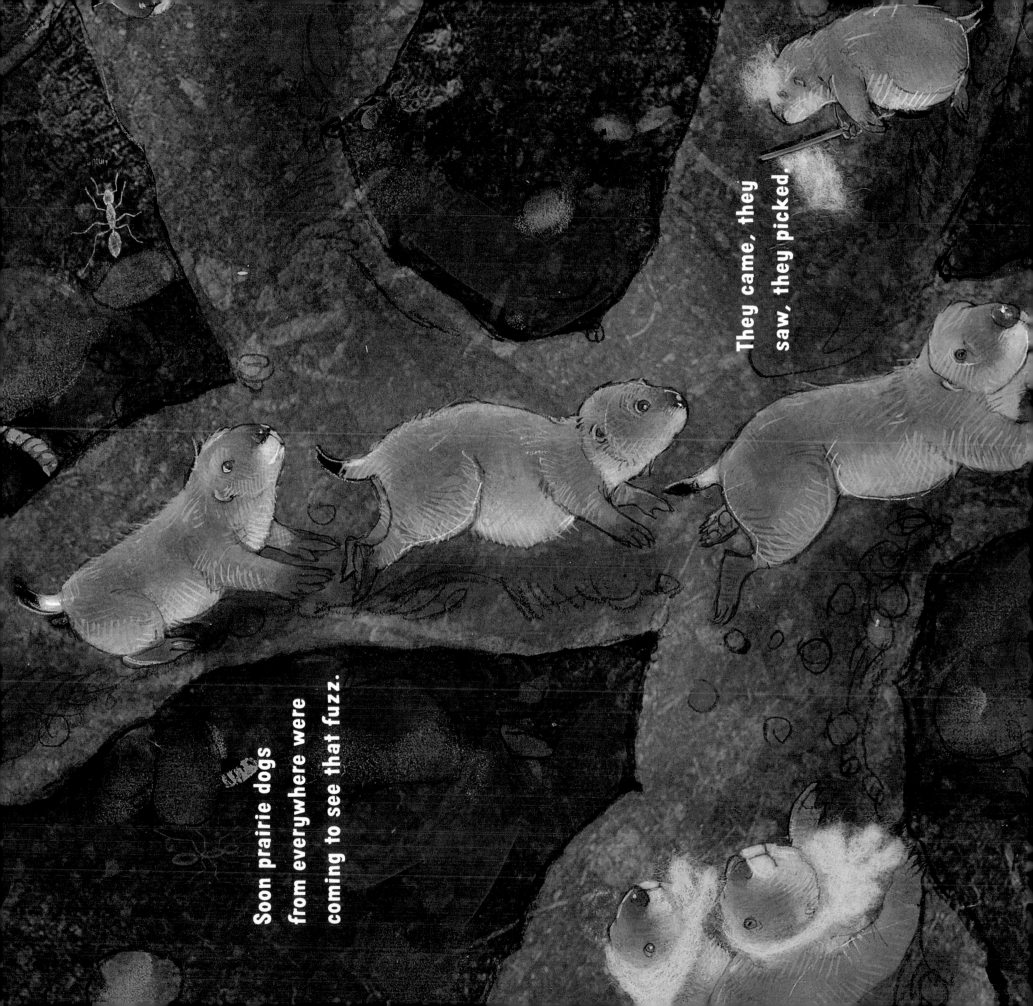

They came, they saw, they picked.

Soon prairie dogs from everywhere were coming to see that fuzz.

They twisted it. Braided it. Danced, and paraded it.
It was a fuzz frenzy.
A fuzz fiesta.
A fuzz fandangle.
The whole prairie was abuzz about fuzz.

They picked and pruned and pulled and pinched.
They pinched and pulled and pruned and picked.

Until . . .
the fuzz ran out.

That big round thing was fuzzless. Naked as a plucked chicken.

Some prairie dogs got a lot of fuzz. Some got a little. Some got no fuzz at all—and they were mad.

"Give me that fuzz!"
"Why?"
"Because."
"It's my fuzz."
"Well, it *was*!"

"Get that fuzz!"

"GET THAT FUZZ!"

Pulling, grabbing, swiping, nabbing, poking, jabbing—it was war! War between the fuzzes and the fuzz-nots. Their peaceful town was a battleground.

It was a fuzz fight.

A fuzz feud.

A fuzz fiasco.

"I started this," moaned Pip Squeak.
"I have to do something. Everyone!
Stop! Stop fighting!"

But those prairie dogs didn't listen. The battle raged on—friend against friend, cousin against cousin, dog against dog—until no one was left standing.

They were pooped. Fuzzled out. Fast asleep.

Hours later the prairie dogs began to stir.

"Uh-oh!"

"Where's the fuzz?"

"I don't know!"

"Where did it go?"

"SOMEONE HAS STOLEN OUR FUZZ!" cried Pip Squeak.

"I DID!" barked a voice from above.

"I STOLE THE FUZZ!"

The prairie dogs froze. Then they raced up, up, up the long tunnel. There stood Big Bark, covered with fuzz from head to tail.

"I'm king of the fuzz!" he snarled.

"Do you hear me? I'm king of the—"

SWOOP!

The sky went black.

"What happened?"

"Where's Big Bark?"

"Look!"

There he was, high above their heads, dangling from the talons of an eagle.

"No more Big Bark!" the crowd cheered. "Yaaaaaay!"

"Don't *yaaaaaay*! He's one of *us*!" yelled Pip. "We have to save him! How would *you* like to be Eagle's lunch?"

"Noooooo!" the crowd yelled.

"Big Bark, wiggle free!" the prairie dogs shouted.
"Shake loose!"
"Hurry!"
"We'll catch you!"
Big Bark twisted and turned, wormed and squirmed. At last he was free of the fuzz!
"Yaaaaaay!" the crowd cheered.

Big Bark fell faster and faster.
"Noooooo!" Prairie dogs scattered.

"Get back here!" yelled Pip. "Quick!
Make a circle! Hold out your paws!"
They ran left, then right, then left.

PLOP!

"You saved me!" Big Bark cried. "But I stole your fuzz!
Now it's gone forever."

"Good," said Pip Squeak. "Fuzz is *trouble*. Right?"

"Yaaaaaay!" the crowd cheered. Friend hugged friend.
Cousin hugged cousin. Dog hugged dog.

"We don't need fuzz," said Pip. "But with Eagle around,
we do need a watchdog with a big—"

"BAAARRRK!" Big Bark rose up on his hind legs. "Eagle's back! BAAARRRK! This is not a test! BAAARRRK! All dogs below! BAAARRRK!"

"Whew! We made it!"

"That was close!"

"Three cheers for Big Bark, the best watchdog ever!"

"YIP, YIP, YAAAAAAY! YIP, YIP, YAAAAAAY! YIP, YIP, YAAAAAAY!"

"Just doing my job!" Big Bark smiled.

"Are we ever getting tangled up with fuzz again?" cried
Pip Squeak.

"Noooooo!" the crowd yelled. "No more fuzz! No more fuzz!"

And from that day forward, the prairie dogs lived happily—and
fuzzlessly—ever after.

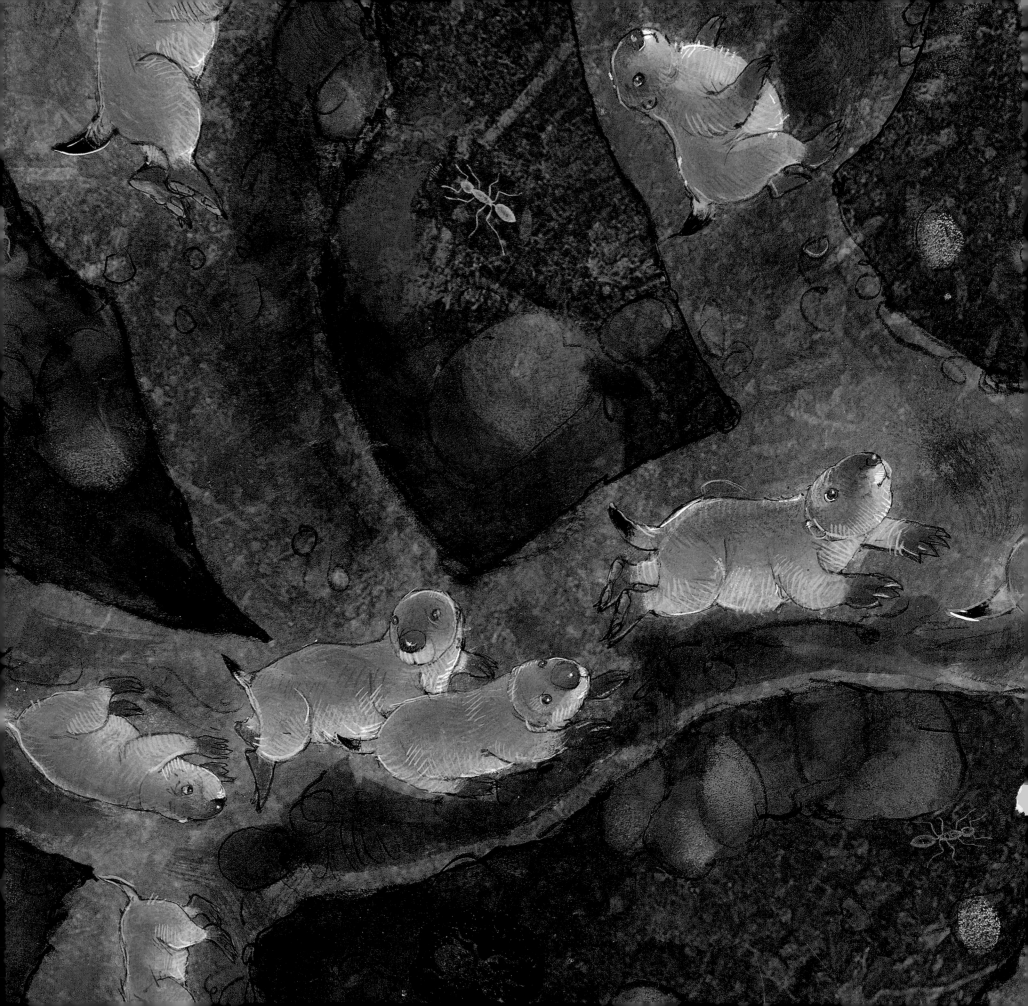

The prairie dogs raced down, down, down the long tunnel.